JOHNNY BOO

"THE BEST LITTLE GHOST IN THE WORLD"

for Eli
& Oliver

CHAPTER ONE:

You can't catch me, Johnny Boo!
Oh yes I can, Squiggle!
I'm too fast!
I've got Squiggle Power!
I'm fast too, because I'm Johnny Boo!
Plus I've got BOO power!

You'll never catch me!
Squiggle power is faster than BOO power.
SWISH DE SWOOSH
No loop-de-loops! That's cheating!
Loop-de-loops aren't cheating
SWOOSH DE SWISH
Yes they are!
No they're not.
SWISH DE SWOOSH
Poor Johnny Boo.
Are you ready to give up?
GRRR...

BOO!
flip
Eek!
Gotcha!
SNATCH
Squiggle power is no match for BOO power.
No fair!
You cheated, Johnny Boo!
If you can use your loop-de-loops then I can go BOO.

I don't care. I'm mad at you now.
Aww... Squiggle.
I'm sorry, I'm sorry!
It's too late for sorries.
I don't want to play with you anymore.
What about double extra sorries?
Hmph!
I'm afraid it's even too late for double extra sorries.
Well... is it too late for ice cream?
Ice cream!?
giggle

Why Johnny Boo, you know it's NEVER too late for ice cream!
HooRay!

CHAPTER TWO:

Come with me, Squiggle.
Okay, Johnny Boo.
Are we going to the ice cream store?
No!
Huh?
Why not Johnny Boo?
I've got some secret ice cream.
Secret ICE CREAM!

Shhh, Squiggle! It's a secret!
Oh, sorry.
Is that why we're whispering?
Yes!
Plus we don't want the ice cream monsters to hear us.
Ice CREAM MONSTERS!
Shh!
But I'm scared of monsters!
Shh, shh. Say it in a WHISPER, Squiggle.

But I'm REALLY scared of monsters, Johnny Boo.
Nice whisper, Squiggle!
Beautiful! Like the sound of wind whispering through the branches of a pine tree on a cold winter's day.
I'm just Really scared.
Oh, poor Squiggle. I'll comfort you.
Poor little cutie.
Don't worry.
Do you know what would Really comfort me, Johnny Boo?
What, Squiggle?
ICE CREAM!

Did someone say ICE CREAM?!
Eek!
An ice cream monster!

CHAPTER THREE:

Go faster, Johnny Boo!
SWISH DE SWOOSH
Use your Squiggle power!
Huff huff
I don't HAVE squiggle power, remember?
Johnny Boo, Johnny Boo! Where are we RUNNING to?
Yow!
BOOM

Well, do Something! He's gonna catch you!
But what what what what what!?
I can't think of anything!
Use your BOO power!
Oh yeah, my BOO power.
Huff huff

BOO!
Oh yeah.
That's the way you do it!
YOW!
Ha ha!
FLOP
That's what I'm talking about, JOHNNY Boo!
Got him!

WAAA!
Gosh, Squiggle.
Waaa!
The monster's crying.
Sob! You scared me, Johnny Boo!
You're a MEAN little ghost!
Hey, I'm not mean!
You're the one who was trying to get us. You're a BAD ice cream monster!
Bad!

I'm not BAD, I'm Nice.
Oh!
You're Nice!?
HooRay!
Wheee!

CHAPTER FOUR:

Now, let's go get that secret ice cream, guys.
Where is it, Johnny Boo?
I don't know...
I've got a squiggley feeling about this.
Here it is. I buried it in the ground!

Oh, dig it up! Dig it up Johnny Boo!
HURRY! HURRY! HURRY UP!
ARE you going to use a shovel, Johnny Boo?
Nope.
Johnny Boo doesn't need a shovel.
Watch this.
BOO!
PLOP

You're cool, Johnny Boo!
See? My secret ice cream.
It's all melted but me and Squiggle like it that way.
Yeah.
Doesn't it look delicious?
Yummy!

You can have the first taste, monster.
Oh Boy!
Let me at it!
Hey.
SNATCH
Gulp!
Ha ha ha ha HA!

Hey! Ice cream monster, you're supposed to SHARE.
Heh heh.
You ate the whole thing! Even the container!
SORRY, Johnny Boo. I just got excited.
There wasn't enough to share.
Ha ha!
Squiggle was RIGHT about you!
Ha ha! SORRY, Johnny Boo.
You're a BAD ice cream monster.
Hey... where is Squiggle, anyhow?
Johnny Boo?

Ice cream monster, you ate Squiggle!
Oops. Sorry!
I didn't mean to.
Johnny Boo, I'm scared!

CHAPTER FIVE:

That's it!
Squiggle! Use your squiggle power!
My squiggle power?
Do some loop-de-loops in there.
And maybe the monster will burp you up.
Uh...
Oh, good IDEA, Johnny Boo!

I don't think I like this idea.
Oh, who asked you?
Are you Ready, Squiggle?
I'm Ready, JohNNy Boo!
ON YOUR mark, get set...
SQUIGGLE!

Go Squiggle Go!
slosh de swoosh
swish de splish
Uh oh!
My tummy tum.
slosh de swish
Loop-de-loops make my tummy UNhappy!
swoosh de slosh

BURP!
Squiggle power!
POP!
Oh! Oh! Oh! I'll catch you!

Woo!
Gotcha!
I was so WORRied about you, Squiggle. ARe you okay?
I think so, Johnny Boo.
In fact, I feel GREAT!
HOORay!
But I don't feel so good... GROAN

CHAPTER SIX:

BURP!
Shhh!
BURP!
Oh, shush.
Stop burping.
BURP!
Be quiet!
Gosh.
BURP! BURP!
BURP! I can't stop burping!
Shhh!
Enough already!
I don't think that he can help it, Squiggle.

My tummy tum tum is still doing loop-de-loops!
BURP!
See, Squiggle?
Help!
Gosh, should we help him? Even though he ate me?
But that was just an accident, Squiggle.
You can't stay mad about that.
BURP!
Help!
I guess you're right, Johnny Boo.
BURP! Help!
I can't BURP stop!
Watch this, Squiggle.

BOO!
Yoiks!
You SCARED me, Johnny Boo!
Why?
Hey, wait a minute! My burping has stopped!

Oh, Johnny Boo! You're the best little ghost in the Whole WORLD!
Hooray for me!
Hooray for all of us, Johnny Boo.
Hooray for all of us.

THE END

Hey Squiggle.
The story is over, but there's still more pages.

Who's that baby, Johnny Boo?
He kind of looks like YOU!

A PHOTO OF THE AUTHOR WHEN HE WAS A BABY:

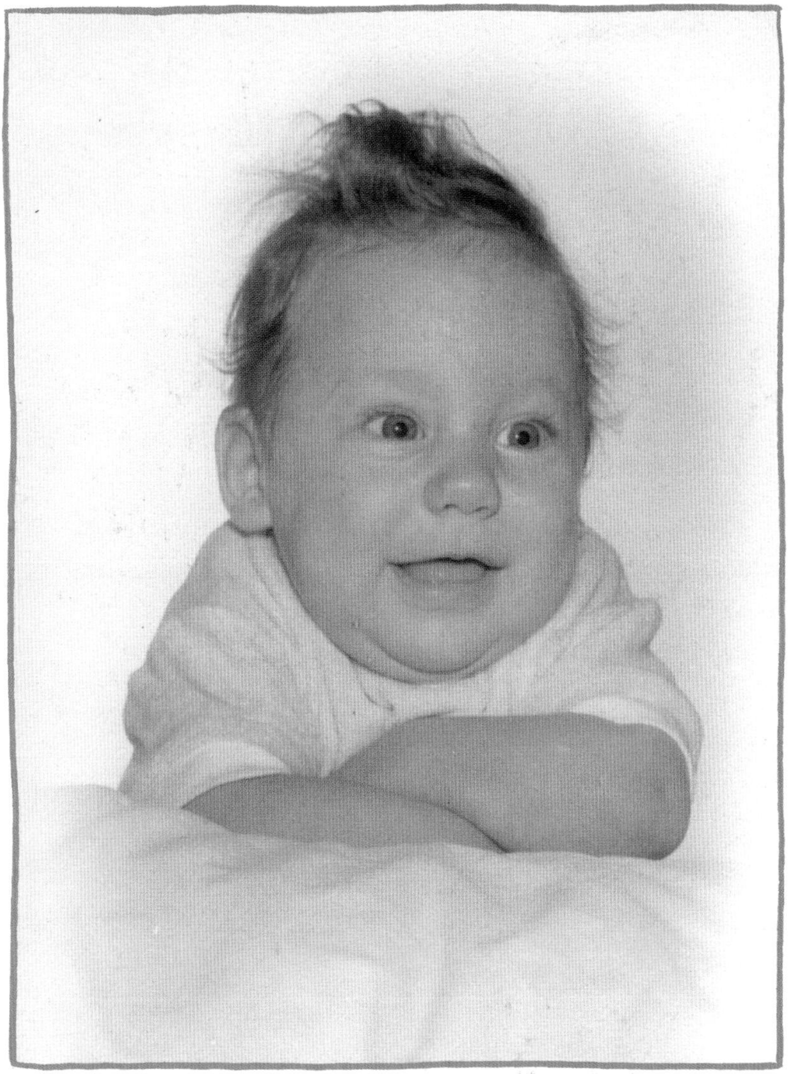